Eagle Warrior

Eagle Warrior

GILL LEWIS

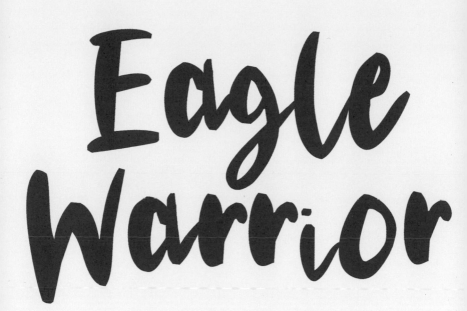

Barrington Stoke

First published in 2019 in Great Britain by
Barrington Stoke Ltd
18 Walker Street, Edinburgh, EH3 7LP

www.barringtonstoke.co.uk

Text © 2019 Gill Lewis
Images © Shutterstock

A CIP catalogue record for this book is available
from the British Library upon request

ISBN: 978-1-78112-874-9

Printed in China by Leo

For Ruth Tingay

Chapter 1

Everything changed the day Haggis died.

Bobbie had never got on with Haggis. He was Granny's dog. He was old, like Granny. He was small and fierce too, like Granny. He'd bite your ankles if he had half a chance.

But Bobbie hadn't wanted him to die.

Poor Haggis.

It was no way for any animal to die.

*

That morning, Bobbie had walked down the garden path to the shed where Granny lived and knocked on the door.

"Come in," shouted Granny.

Bobbie walked in and sat on the end of Granny's bed. Haggis watched Bobbie and growled rude dog words at her from his basket beside the wood-burner.

Granny lived in the garden shed. It was more like a summerhouse. It had big windows that looked out across the fields to the moorland and mountains. There was a bed, an armchair and a table, and that was it. Dad had put a wood-burning stove inside to keep her warm through the winters. Outside, she had a small campfire with a ring of stones around it and two old deckchairs to sit in. There were candles in jam jars hanging like fairy lights along the branches of a tree.

She said she wouldn't live anywhere else.

She was Granny Mountain.

She even looked like a mountain. Her face was full of wrinkles, like a craggy rock. She had wisps of snow-white hair on top of her head. She stomped in her big boots across the Scottish hills as if she was a mini mountain troll.

"Are you coming up on the hill today, Granny?" said Bobbie.

Granny scowled and pulled on her blue woollen coat. It was the one she wore if she went to town. "Your mum says I've got to have my flu jab today. I missed it last year and there's flu going round."

"In summer?" said Bobbie.

"So it seems," said Granny. "Your mum says I have to go."

"I'll look out for our eagle for you," said Bobbie. "I'm going up the hill to see if he's still there."

Granny stood by the window and looked out at the dark-green block of forest at the edge of the farm. "I reckon he's having a lie-in," she said. "I haven't seen him flying about yet this morning."

Bobbie got up to go. "I'll say hello to him for you."

"You'll need these," Granny told Bobbie. She looped the strap of the binoculars over Bobbie's neck. "You can take Haggis with you too."

Bobbie and Haggis looked hard at each other.

Haggis growled softly.

"I don't think Haggis wants to come with me," said Bobbie. She didn't want Granny to know that she didn't want to take him.

"He doesn't like being left on his own," Granny said as she pushed them both out of the door. "Now shoo, both of you."

Haggis grumbled, but he trotted after Bobbie on his stiff little legs as she went through the farmyard and out across the hill. The sheep and lambs moved away from them as they made their way up the track that led to open moorland. Only Mavis, Bobbie's hand-fed lamb, bleated sadly after her.

The sky was bright blue but a cool breeze was blowing and so Bobbie zipped up her coat. It was her favourite coat. It had been a present from Granny nearly a year ago for her tenth birthday. Bobbie loved it. It had lots of pockets. It had pockets inside pockets. It even had pockets inside pockets inside pockets. She could hide a whole packet of biscuits without Mum seeing. It was the best sort of coat.

Bobbie crossed over the footbridge and waited for Haggis to catch up with her. She looked back to the small farmhouse and the fields dotted with sheep. Her own small flock was mixed in with Dad's sheep, but she knew all hers by name. The farm was home. It sat in a valley in the middle of land owned by Charles Hunt, the 10th Duke of Glen-Gallows. The Duke owned the moorland and mountains as far as the eye could see.

Bobbie climbed up to the top of the small hill and sat down between the rocks, out of the cold wind. She could see Haggis below, sniffing through the heather for rabbits. She munched on a biscuit and held the binoculars to her eyes.

She and Granny had been watching a golden
eagle for the last three days. They had seen
it flying high up in the sky. It soared with its
wings spread wide. It was a huge bird. Each
night it had come to roost in the trees at the
forest edge. Bobbie scanned the trees until
she found the eagle resting near the top of
its favourite pine tree. It was hard to believe
that something so big and fierce could be here
on their farm. Granny said it was probably a
young one that was looking for a new place to
live. In the early morning sunlight, its feathers
shone in all the colours of brown from gold
to dark chocolate. Its curved beak was the
colour of steel and its bright yellow feet curled
around the branch. It was awake and watching
something up in the sky.

Loud croaks above made Bobbie look up.
Two ravens sailed above her. Their feathers
shone black and gun-metal blue. They had
seen the eagle too, and she watched them spin

downwards and dive-bomb it. The eagle spread his huge wings and flew upwards, flapping hard in the still air between the trees. He caught the wind above the treetops and vanished away across the moor. The two ravens mobbed him as he went.

She hoped the ravens hadn't chased the eagle away for good. She'd have to ask Granny about them.

Bobbie finished her biscuit and looked around for Haggis.

"Haggis," she called.

But she couldn't see Haggis anywhere.

Sometimes he pretended not to hear.

Bobbie climbed down from the rocks and set off to look for him.

She could see him on the other side of a stream, eating something on the ground.

"Ugh, Haggis, drop it," said Bobbie.

Haggis kept munching at a very dead, very smelly rabbit.

"Haggis, that's gross," shouted Bobbie as she marched towards him. "Leave it."

Haggis took a few steps back.

He didn't look quite right.

His legs tottered and he stumbled.

He vomited.

He gave a little whimper.

Then he dropped down.

Dead.

Chapter 2

"Haggis?" whispered Bobbie as she took a step closer towards him.

Bobbie had been a farmer's daughter long enough to know a dead animal from a living one and Haggis was most definitely dead. But this was Granny's dog. Granny loved her dog.

Haggis's fur was covered in dog sick, and Bobbie didn't want to touch him. Instead, she took off her coat, scooped Haggis inside it and lifted him up.

Despite his small size, he was solid and chunky and very heavy.

She held him closer than she had ever done before and carried him home, feeling the sadness like a heavy weight inside her heart.

As she walked to the farmhouse, she could see Mum's car pulling up in the drive.

Granny got out first. "What is it, Bobbie?"

"Oh, Granny," said Bobbie. And she couldn't stop the tears from falling. "It's Haggis. He's dead."

Granny lifted the corner of Bobbie's coat. "Poor wee man. What happened?"

"He was eating an old dead rabbit, and then he just died. It was so quick."

Granny's eyes opened wide. "Where was this?"

"Out on the hill, Granny. Near the tree where we see the eagle."

Granny said some rude words that Bobbie knew she wasn't allowed to repeat. Mum called it Granny's blue talk.

"I'm sorry, Granny, I couldn't stop him," said Bobbie.

Granny's rude words were electric blue and shot like lightning from her mouth.

She snatched the coat with Haggis inside it, lifted the lid of the wheelie bin and dumped him inside, coat and all.

"Granny!" was all Bobbie could say. "That's my best coat."

"Did you touch him?" shouted Granny.

"What?"

"Did you touch Haggis? Did you touch the rabbit?"

"No, Granny," said Bobbie.

Granny grabbed Bobbie by the arm and pulled her into the kitchen.

"Granny, you're hurting me," said Bobbie.

"Wash your hands!" snapped Granny. "Now!"

Mum followed them in. "What are you doing?"

Granny turned on the tap and pulled Bobbie's hands under the running water. "Are you sure you didn't touch him?"

"Yes, Granny."

Dad came through the door. "What's all the noise? What's happened?"

"It's Haggis," said Granny, spitting words like she was spitting teeth. "He's been poisoned." She turned to face Mum and Dad. "And if Bobbie had even touched that poison with her bare hands, she'd be dead like Haggis too."

Chapter 3

"Poison?" said Dad. "Are you sure?"

"Yes," said Granny. "There's been an eagle over the moor. Don't tell me you've forgotten what happened to the last eagle here?"

"No," said Dad quietly.

"What do you mean?" asked Bobbie. "What happened to the eagle?"

Her granny explained that four years ago, when Bobbie was six, an eagle had been found poisoned on the duke's land.

"Why would anyone poison an eagle?" asked Bobbie.

"For the same reason they shoot the foxes and kill the crows and ravens," Granny told her. "The duke doesn't want eagles because they eat his red grouse."

There were lots of red grouse on the moor. They were wild birds a bit like chickens, and rich people paid thousands of pounds to come and shoot them.

"The duke puts poison out?" said Bobbie.

"Well, not him," said Granny. "Angus, his gamekeeper, does it for him."

Dad frowned. "We don't know that," he said. "There was no proof the last time."

"Exactly, and that's the problem," said Granny. "But tell me who else round here wants eagles killed?"

Bobbie dried her hands on a towel. "But it's against the law to kill an eagle," she said.

"I know," said Granny. "Isn't that the truth?!"

Mum poured boiling water into the teapot and opened a tin of biscuits. "I reckon we all need a cup of tea," she said.

"We'll have to tell the police about Haggis," said Bobbie.

Granny looked at Mum. "Bobbie's right, you know. And it could have been her who was poisoned."

Dad took a biscuit and broke it in two. "I'll have a word with Angus first."

"A word?" said Granny. "A word!" She glared at Dad. "It's probably him who put the poison out."

Bobbie's mum put her hand on Granny's arm. "Mum, it's best to sort this out without calling the police."

"Why?" asked Bobbie.

Granny pulled her arm away. "Because we don't want to upset the neighbours, especially when one's a duke."

"It's not like that," said Dad.

Granny took a big slurp of tea. "Isn't it?"

"I said I'll have a word with Angus," said Dad. "Let's keep the police out of this." He stormed out and slammed the door behind him.

Bobbie turned to Granny. "What about Haggis?"

Granny sat down. All at once the anger was gone and she looked sad. "We'll dig a hole. A deep one. We'll bury your coat with him an' all." She sniffed loudly. "Poor Haggis. He was a fierce wee beastie," she said, "but he was *my* fierce beastie. He didn't deserve to die like that."

*

Granny didn't turn up at suppertime and Mum told Bobbie to leave Granny alone for a while. Bobbie went to bed with her window wide open. The summer night was damp with dew and the air smelled of pine and heather. Stars began to sprinkle across the sky. Bobbie could see Granny sitting outside, staring out across the mountains that she had once walked with Haggis.

Beside Granny, the glow from one lone candle burned long into the night.

Chapter 4

Bobbie woke to the sound of Mum and Granny arguing downstairs.

"Why didn't you tell me before?" shouted Granny. "As if Haggis dying wasn't bad enough, now you tell me more bad news!"

Bobbie pulled on her dressing gown and ran downstairs into the kitchen. "What's happened?"

Granny was stirring a pan of porridge. Bobbie could see how angry she was.

Bobbie's mum sighed and turned to face Granny. "We've got no choice. Your brother has had a bad fall and can't look after himself. We're his only family. He's coming here for a bit and that's the end of it."

Bobbie sat down at the table. "Is Uncle Fraser coming to stay?"

"Yes," said Mum. "Your dad left early to fetch him from Edinburgh. Uncle Fraser can have the spare room."

"Pfff!" huffed Granny. "He'll expect you to roll out a red carpet for him so he doesn't step in the mud. You'll be getting all posh with napkins out and we'll have to drink tea from teacups and saucers."

Bobbie's mum wagged her finger at Granny. "You have to behave, Mum. Uncle Fraser is your brother and he doesn't have anyone else.

You have to try to get on. If he likes drinking from teacups, that's fine."

"Hmph," said Granny. "Nothing wrong with a mug." She poured her porridge into a bowl and stomped outside. "If you want to see the eagle, Bobbie, come and see me after breakfast. I'll be in my shed where it's cold and damp, not warm and dry like the spare room that Fraser will have."

Mum shut the door. "Granny doesn't even want the spare room," she said. "She just likes to make a fuss."

Bobbie smiled and sprinkled salt on her porridge. "I hope Uncle Fraser brings some of his books."

Uncle Fraser was Bobbie's great uncle, but she'd always called him Uncle Fraser. He used to be in charge of a museum in Edinburgh and his house was full of books on every subject from cave paintings to modern cities. He dressed the same every day, in a tweed suit with a waistcoat and silk scarf. His shoes were polished leather. In one pocket he kept a pocket watch that was a hundred years old, and in the other he had the latest smart phone. Bobbie was secretly excited that he was coming. He always came for Christmas and brought interesting presents. Last year he taught her to play chess and gave her a replica of the Lewis Chessmen, one of the oldest chess sets in the world. Bobbie loved the chessmen's grumpy and scary faces.

"I'm sure he'll bring some of his books," said Mum. "He'll need them. There's not much for him to do here."

Bobbie sighed. "Why don't Granny and Uncle Fraser get on?"

Mum sat down and took a sip of tea. "I'm sure you've heard Granny's side of the story before. When they were children, it was just after the war and there wasn't a teacher at their local school, so it had to shut. Their parents could only afford to send one of their children away to boarding school, so they decided to send Uncle Fraser because he was the boy. He went on to university and travelled the world studying ancient history. Granny had to stay at home on the farm. She married your grampa, who was a local shepherd. When Grampa died, your dad and I took over the farm."

"But Granny loves it here," said Bobbie. "She wouldn't want to live in the city."

"I know," said Mum. "But I think she feels bitter that she didn't have a choice and Uncle Fraser did."

"You would never think they were brother and sister," said Bobbie.

"I know," sighed Mum. "I've never met two people that are more different in my life."

*

Granny was waiting for Bobbie outside her shed. "Thought you'd never come," she snapped.

Granny looked so cross that it was almost as if there was a thunderstorm above her head with bolts of lightning shooting out. Bobbie wasn't sure if Granny was upset about Haggis or the news that Uncle Fraser was coming to stay – or both.

As they walked across the fields together, Granny stopped being so moody. She always got better once she was outside. Granny belonged on the mountain.

"How are your sheep doing?" asked Granny after they'd been walking a little while.

"I'm keeping two of the lambs this year," said Bobbie. "Then I'll have my own flock of ten."

"You'll be needing a sheepdog of your own to help you soon," said Granny.

Bobbie smiled. "D'you think Dad would let me have one?"

"Ha!" said Granny. "We'll work on him. His dog could do with some help."

"I'd like one from a pup so I can train it myself. You'd help me, wouldn't you, Granny?"

"If you want me to," Granny said. "Did I tell you about the time I won the county sheepdog trials with my dog, Floss?"

Bobbie pushed her hands deep in her pockets. Granny had told her that story a thousand times, but she still loved hearing it. She and Granny walked along by a small stream at the edge of the forest and Bobbie listened happily to the story of Granny and Floss and their victory over the McKenzie brothers. Bobbie was dreaming about having a sheepdog of her own, so she didn't notice Granny had stopped, and she almost bumped into her.

"Look, there's the eagle. It's on a different tree," said Granny.

They both stopped and Bobbie put the binoculars to her eyes for a better view. It was closer this time, with its back to them. There was a long wire sticking out from its back. "It's got something stuck to it," said Bobbie.

Granny took the binoculars from her. "Ooh!" said Granny. "I hadn't noticed that before. I think it's got a satellite tag. I heard a programme about that on the radio. The tag sends a signal so that the eagle watchers know exactly where it is."

"Eagle watchers?" said Bobbie.

"Yes," said Granny. "They're the scientific folk who track these eagles."

"That's good, isn't it?" said Bobbie. "It means someone's looking out for it."

"Sort of," said Granny. "It doesn't stop someone putting poison out, but if it does get poisoned, then its tag will stop moving and the eagle watchers will come and find it."

"But what if Angus smashes up the tag because he doesn't want them to find it?" asked Bobbie. "What if it can't send a signal?"

Granny frowned. "Then I suppose the eagle will just vanish without a trace."

"Speaking of Angus," said Bobbie as she peered through the trees. "Isn't that him over there?"

Granny looked through the trees too. Angus was walking along a track, keeping to the shadows. He was a tall thin man, with dark hair and pale skin. He wore a dark-green jacket and carried a shotgun under his arm. He was looking up at the treetops.

"C'mon," said Granny as she stuffed the binoculars under her coat. "My guess is that he's seen the eagle flying about here but doesn't know where it's roosting. We don't want him to find it. You stay here. I'm going to distract him."

"Granny!" called Bobbie. She ran to catch up.

Angus saw them and scowled.

"You're out of your way," Granny said to Angus. "Don't normally see you here in the forest."

"I'm counting red grouse on this side of the moor," Angus said.

"How odd," said Granny. "They don't roost in the tops of trees. Not looking for anything else, are you?"

Angus ignored her and walked over to his quad bike.

Granny followed him. "My dog was poisoned yesterday. I've got a funny feeling you might know something about it."

"Not me," said Angus. He sneered. "But it's no bad thing that dog's gone. He was an ugly old mutt."

"Bobbie found him," said Granny, her voice getting louder. "Poison like that could have killed her too. How would you feel about the death of a child?"

Angus looked quickly back at Bobbie and started up the engine. "Move out of my way. You've got no proof."

Granny hadn't finished. "If I find any more dead rabbits that have been put out as poisoned bait, I'm calling the police."

"That wouldn't be a good idea," said Angus, revving the engine. "You don't want to make an enemy of the duke."

Granny put her hands on her hips. "You don't scare me. It's time you lot stopped killing eagles. You should go to prison for what you've done."

Angus drove the quad bike forward so that it almost touched Granny. "You don't scare me either," he said. "No one has ever been arrested for killing an eagle. There's nothing you can do."

"You're right," spat Granny. "People like you and the duke get away with it all the time. And that's the biggest crime of all."

Chapter 5

Uncle Fraser arrived in the evening as the sun was setting. Bobbie ran out to see him and help bring his bags into the house. She couldn't find any shoes to put on, so she hopped across the gravel in her bare feet.

Dad helped Uncle Fraser out of the car and handed him his crutches.

"Uncle Fraser!" said Bobbie.

"Bobbie!" Uncle Fraser smiled. "My favourite great niece."

Bobbie laughed. "I'm your only great niece."

Uncle Fraser peered closely at her. "Let's have a look at you. A bit taller. A bit older." He looked down at her feet. "Oh dear," he said, shaking his head. "This won't do. You are getting as wild as your granny. We'll have to do something about it."

Bobbie laughed. "Have you brought any books, Uncle Fraser?"

He nodded to one of his bags. "Try lifting that one."

Bobbie tried to lift it, but it was so heavy that she couldn't even get it off the ground.

"It's full of books to keep me busy," said Uncle Fraser. "There are a few I think you'll like too."

At suppertime, Bobbie sat between Granny and Uncle Fraser, not sure which one to talk to in case she upset the other.

Mum spooned lamb stew onto plates. "It's good to see you, Uncle Fraser," she said.

Uncle Fraser tucked his napkin into his shirt. "Thank you, Fiona. This looks delicious, as usual. It's kind of you to let me stay."

"My pleasure." Mum smiled.

Granny picked up a fork and inspected it. "Are these the silver ones, dear? We don't usually see these ones out unless we have a special guest."

Mum gave Granny a hard look. "Uncle Fraser *is* a special guest."

Granny lifted a wine glass and inspected it. "Wine and crystal glasses too. We are going up in the world."

Uncle Fraser ignored Granny and turned to Bobbie. "So, Bobbie, how's school?"

Bobbie didn't know what to say. Why did adults always ask about school? "Fine," she said.

"I mean what are your favourite subjects? Science? English? History?"

Bobbie looked down at her food.

Uncle Fraser took a sip of wine. "What's your dream, Bobbie? What do you wish most for in the world?"

Bobbie turned to Dad. Maybe this was the moment. "I want a dog."

"A dog?" said Uncle Fraser. His bushy eyebrows shot up.

"A dog?'" said Dad.

Bobbie nodded. "A sheepdog of my own. I want a pup to train."

Uncle Fraser smiled. "I mean what are your dreams for your future?"

Mum turned to Bobbie. "Uncle Fraser has made us a very generous offer. He wants to pay for you to go to St Rhona's School for Girls."

"St Rhona's?" said Bobbie.

Dad nodded. "It's a very good school in Edinburgh. You could board there in the term time."

"They get very good results," said Mum. "It would be a wonderful chance for you."

"I like it here," said Bobbie.

Uncle Fraser dabbed his mouth with his napkin. "In Edinburgh you have the theatre and museums and the art galleries. There's so much to see," he said. He opened his arms wide. "There's culture."

Granny did the biggest burp Bobbie had
ever heard. Bobbie saw Granny's mouth curl up
in a smile and she knew Granny had done it on
purpose.

"I have indigestion tablets if you need
some," said Uncle Fraser.

"No need for that," said Granny. She did
another loud burp. "Better out than in."

Uncle Fraser frowned. "If I were you, I'd see
a doctor, my dear."

They ate in silence after that, the knives
and forks tapping on the plates.

"Pudding, anyone?" said Mum. "It's apple
tart."

"Pudding too?" said Granny, raising her
eyebrows. "Well, this is a treat. I can't
remember the last time I had pudding."

"I'm a little full, thank you," said Uncle Fraser. He looked over at Granny. "And I've had better company. Maybe I could have pudding in my room with a cup of tea later. Earl Grey tea, if you have it."

Bobbie watched Dad help Uncle Fraser up the stairs.

Granny shook her head. "Bobbie doesn't need museums and galleries when she's got all this," she said, pointing out of the window to the mountains.

"Granny!" said Bobbie's mum. "It's very good of Uncle Fraser to offer to pay for St Rhona's. You said you wished you'd had the chances he had. Maybe he's trying to make up for it with Bobbie."

Granny scowled and got up to leave. She imitated Uncle Fraser's posh Edinburgh accent.

"I'm a little full too, Fiona dear," she said, dabbing her napkin on her lips. "Maybe I could have apple tart brought to me in my cold damp shed with a cup of tea." With that, she stomped out of the house.

Bobbie waited until Dad came back into the kitchen. "I don't want to go to a different school."

"It's a very good school," said Mum.

"I like it here," said Bobbie.

"Have a think about it," said Dad. "It can't hurt to think about it."

But it did hurt to think about it, because it would mean leaving the farm, leaving Mum, Dad and Granny, and leaving her eagle.

Chapter 6

That evening, Bobbie didn't go out to see Granny. Instead, she took the tea and apple tart to Uncle Fraser. She didn't want to talk about the new school, so she sat with him and told him all about the eagle instead.

"We had a show about eagles at the museum once," said Uncle Fraser. "It was wonderful. There were sculptures and paintings and ancient jewellery in the shape of eagles. People have worshipped eagles for thousands of years."

"Not here," said Bobbie. "People want to kill them."

"Well, that's a shame," said Uncle Fraser. He pointed to one of the bags he had brought with him. "Have a look in there, Bobbie. There's a book about people who hunt with eagles in Mongolia."

Bobbie pulled out a large book and opened it at a page with a photo of a hunter wearing furs and bright clothes. He was riding a horse and he had an eagle on his arm.

"The Kazakh nomads hunt with golden eagles," said Uncle Fraser. "They catch the eagles when they're young, then they train them to hunt. But after about eight years, they return them to the wild again."

Bobbie turned the pages to look at pictures of eagles soaring above a vast landscape of plains and mountains. It was like opening a window to a different world. *What would it be*

like to hold an eagle and train it to fly for you?
she thought.

Mum stuck her head around the door.
"Bedtime," she said. "Let Uncle Fraser get some
rest."

Bobbie gave Uncle Fraser a hug and went
out. "I'll go and say goodnight to Granny too,"
she told Mum.

"Granny's asleep," said Mum. "You can see
her in the morning."

Bobbie brushed her teeth and got ready for
bed. She switched the light off and opened the
window wide. She curled up under her duvet
and stared out at the crescent moon. The
moonlight on her duvet made it look as if the
folds were a range of snowy mountains. Bobbie
linked her thumbs together and spread her

fingers wide, as if they were wings, and made her hands fly over the duvet mountains.

Soon she was asleep. She dreamed she was flying high above the earth, with the wind in her wings. The valley lay far below, with the river glittering in the evening sunlight. Her wingtips touched the thin wisps of cloud that curled in the thin air. This was her world – of wild open sky.

A single gunshot rang out.

She felt the shot. Suddenly the air no longer held her. She was falling towards the earth. The ground rushed up towards her, the heather and rocks came closer and closer. Her tattered wings trailed behind her.

She was falling,
falling,
falling.

Bobbie sat up in bed gasping for breath. She gripped onto the bed. She was wide awake, heart banging in her chest.

A horrible dream.

A horrible dream.

She lay back in bed, her hands clammy with sweat.

She lay still and tried to forget her dream.

Another shot rang out.

It shattered the silence. Startled crows cawed loudly as they took flight.

Bobbie was up and out of bed, staring out of the window.

The moorland was dark and still.

But somewhere out there, someone had fired two shots into the night.

Chapter 7

Bobbie saw Granny's light come on inside her shed.

Granny must have heard the shots too.

Bobbie grabbed her phone, dressed quickly and crept downstairs and out of the back door. Granny was standing beside her shed looking over to the forest edge.

"You heard it too?" said Bobbie.

"Yes," said Granny.

"Who'd be out this time of night?" said Bobbie.

"Who d'you think?" growled Granny. "Those shots came from the forest edge where the eagle roosts. Though I don't know how Angus could shoot an eagle in the dark."

"Maybe he's got one of those night-vision cameras," said Bobbie. "The ones that pick up body heat. You see them on the TV in wildlife programmes or when policemen catch burglars at night."

Granny was silent for a time. "I wish I had one of those cameras to look for whoever's out there shooting eagles."

"We could go out now and look," said Bobbie.

Granny shook her head. "There's no point. We won't see anything. We'll go at first light."

Bobbie curled up with a blanket in Granny's armchair, but she couldn't sleep. She stayed awake and watched the stars fade and the dawn sky turn blood red.

Had Angus really shot the eagle? She didn't want to believe that the eagle she and Granny had watched soar over the mountains might already be dead.

*

As the first rays of sun lit up the sky, Granny yawned and stretched. She hadn't slept much either. "Let's go then," she said. "But I don't think we'll find anything. If Angus has killed the eagle, he'll have hidden it and will be far away already."

"What would he do with it?" said Bobbie.

"He'd probably destroy the tag and bury the eagle somewhere," said Granny. "Its last signal will have been sent from here."

"So the eagle watchers might come here, if they think this is the last place he roosted," said Bobbie. "We can tell them we heard two shots."

"There's no proof," snapped Granny. "And that's the problem. Angus would say the shots were him out shooting foxes."

Bobbie and Granny walked across the fields. Rain was in the air. Bobbie could feel it. Dark clouds had spread across the sky. A storm was brewing up in the mountains.

Bobbie scanned the treetops. She hoped and hoped to see the eagle but couldn't spot him anywhere.

The wind rose and rushed through the trees, and above that came the sound of an engine.

"Shh!" said Bobbie, and pulled Granny into the shadows. "There's Angus on his quad bike."

They both crouched down and watched Angus switch the engine off and let his dog jump down. Angus began to scan the trees with his binoculars while he sent his dog away into the brambles. He walked up and down the track as if he was looking for something.

"What's he doing here?" whispered Bobbie.

Granny peered out. "He's looking for the eagle, of course. I think he shot it but didn't kill it. It might be injured somewhere. He could be in trouble if the eagle watchers find it has been shot."

Bobbie stood up and brushed the pine needles from her jeans. "Let's find the eagle before Angus does."

"Come on," said Granny. "Let's put him off." She stomped through bracken towards Angus.

Angus spun around. He couldn't hide the surprise on his face before he scowled at them. "What're you doing here?"

"We heard shots in the night," said Granny. "Thought we'd come and look."

Angus just watched her.

"Looking for something, Angus?" said Granny. "An eagle, perhaps?"

Angus spat on the ground. "Why don't you go and mind your own business?"

"This *is* my business," snapped Granny.

"Mine too," said Bobbie, stepping forward.

Angus glared at them, then turned and headed up the track, sending his dog into the forest again.

"Let's go this way," said Bobbie. "Let's find the eagle before he does."

Bobbie and Granny headed back along the southern edge of the forest, looking up into the branches and down across the forest floor. But it was difficult to see into the green gloom.

After nearly two hours of walking and looking, Granny sat down on a log. Angus had already driven away, but it didn't look like he had found the eagle either.

"Where d'you think it is?" asked Bobbie.

Granny shook her head. "No idea."

It was as if their eagle had vanished into thin air.

Chapter 8

Bobbie and Granny headed back to the farmhouse.

"If it's hurt and has stopped moving, the eagle watchers will come and try to find it," said Granny.

"How long will that take?" asked Bobbie.

Granny shrugged her shoulders. "I don't know."

"I'm going back out after breakfast to look for it," said Bobbie. "I want to find it before Angus does."

Bobbie's stomach rumbled. She had been out since dawn and was starving. She could see the yellow glow of the light in the kitchen and Uncle Fraser sitting at the table.

A scowl crept across Granny's face. "I forgot he was still here. I expect he's having smoked salmon for his breakfast."

Bobbie kicked off her boots by the door and went inside; Granny held the door open. Uncle Fraser was wearing a silk dressing gown, spreading toast with butter and jam. He was looking at his phone.

"They're rude, those things are," said Granny. "People spend their lives looking at their phones and forget to look around them."

"I'd still be lying on the floor if I hadn't had my phone with me to call the ambulance," said Uncle Fraser. "Even better, I can keep in contact with Bobbie too."

"Well, I don't need to phone her," said Granny. "She can hear me yelling across the farm."

"She could probably hear you yelling in Edinburgh," Dad muttered under his breath.

"If she goes to St Rhona's, you'll need a phone to speak to her," said Uncle Fraser.

Granny glowered at Uncle Fraser. "Well, she's not going."

"Says who?" said Uncle Fraser.

Granny puffed out her chest. "Bobbie's life is here, on the mountains with the moors and eagles, not in some boring city."

"Boring?" snapped Uncle Fraser, pointing his butter knife at her. "And what's here? Just sheep and heather. What will she know of the world if she stays here?"

Granny wagged her finger at Uncle Fraser. "And you'd have her head filled with books and nonsense and she'd forget to live," she shouted.

Uncle Fraser banged his teacup down so hard that tea slopped over the table. "I thought you'd want Bobbie to have the chances you didn't have," he said angrily. "You're not exactly a great example for her. I've never seen you read a book in your life."

"Stop it!" cried Bobbie. "Both of you. I'm sick of it."

Granny and Uncle Fraser turned to her, stunned.

"Just stop it." Bobbie got up to leave. "I'm going out."

"Wait," said Granny. "I'll come with you."

"No," snapped Bobbie. "I'm going out. Alone."

Chapter 9

Bobbie grabbed Dad's coat, pulled on her trainers and ran.

She wanted to be away from everyone and everything.

She let her feet carry her. Instead of running towards the forest, she headed out over the moor, following the rutted paths up between the heather. She knew every curve of these hills and each stream and valley. She slowed down to a walk now that she was away from the farmhouse. A cold blast of wind warned her there was rain coming. She looked ahead to see the curtain of rain trailing towards her.

She could see someone else was out on the moor too, working his way up the valley. It was Angus. He looked like he was searching for something. For the eagle, Bobbie guessed.

So maybe the eagle was hurt. Maybe it had taken flight after Angus had fired at it. She tried to think what she would have done if she were an eagle. Where would she have looked for shelter? She looked along the valley into the soft folds of woodland by the river. *There,* she thought. *That's where I'd go.*

The rain began to fall cold and hard. It seeped through her collar and down her shirt. Her trainers were soaked through and her feet felt like blocks of ice. She headed to the river, to the place Granny and she called the Otter Pools, because they had once seen an otter playing there. She knew there was an overhang of rock she could shelter beneath.

On the other side of the river she could see Angus making his way upstream. She didn't want him to see her, so she scrambled down the bank, holding onto a twisted old rowan tree. Granny had always said that rowan trees had magic in them. They could protect you from evil. She told fairy tales about people who climbed into a rowan tree to escape the devil.

Bobbie crouched low behind the tree but then let out a gasp.

A huge bird was caught in the fork of the rowan tree. It hung limp in the branches. The golden feathers on its neck had lost their shine and were soaked and matted together. It looked like it had just fallen out of the sky.

It was the eagle.

Bobbie reached up to touch it and it blinked and opened its mouth.

It was alive.

It was even bigger close up. It was watching her with dark-brown eyes that were flecked with gold. One wing was pinned back and trapped in the branches. Bobbie tried to lift it, and as she did, it beat its wings in her face and a sharp talon pierced her coat.

She didn't think she could do it on her own.

It was hurt.

It needed help.

The rain was coming down faster now and splashing off the ground. She took off Dad's coat and tried to cover the eagle. The rain seeped into her jumper and soon she was shivering with cold. She didn't want to leave the eagle alone because Angus might find it before she returned with help.

If only Granny were here. She'd know what to do.

Bobbie pulled her phone from her pocket. She rang Mum and then Dad, but there was no answer. There wasn't much charge left on her phone. Granny didn't have a phone. That left Uncle Fraser.

She pressed his number.

"Uncle Fraser?"

"Yes? Is that you, Bobbie?"

"Can you get Granny for me?"

There was silence. Then, "I'm not speaking to her and she doesn't want to speak to me."

"Please, Uncle Fraser."

"Not until she says sorry," said Uncle Fraser.

"Uncle Fraser. This is an emergency," Bobbie begged. "Tell her I've found the eagle at the Otter Pools. It's alive but it's hurt. I'm scared because Angus is somewhere here too."

"Bobbie ... I ..."

But Bobbie's phone lost charge and died.

Bobbie threw it to the ground.

She turned to look at the eagle, but its head hung limp again.

"Don't die," she whispered. "Please don't die."

But the eagle closed its eyes. Its breathing became short and shallow.

Everything was going wrong.

She felt helpless and alone.

She couldn't hold on to anything any more.

Mum and Dad wanted her to go to a different school.

Everything was changing, and she couldn't seem to stop it.

She was losing her eagle and being sent far from her home.

Chapter 10

"Bobbie? Are you there, Bobbie?"

"Granny?" called Bobbie. "Is that you?"

Bobbie looked up and saw Granny's feet above her on the riverbank. She slipped down the bank to where Bobbie sat. Dad was with her.

"You're freezing," said Granny.

"So is the eagle," said Bobbie.

Dad pulled another jumper and coat from his rucksack for Bobbie and a blanket to wrap around the eagle. He and Granny untangled the eagle from the tree and Bobbie softly wrapped the blanket around it.

"Uncle Fraser gave you the message?" said Bobbie.

Granny looked a bit embarrassed. "I'm afraid I ignored him until he hammered on my door and shouted at me that you were in trouble."

"He wanted to come too," said Dad. He smiled. "But even if he could walk without crutches, I can't see him out here somehow."

"He's back at home calling the eagle watchers," said Granny. "He found their number on that phone of his."

"They're coming to the farm?" said Bobbie.

"Yes," said Granny. "They'll take care of our eagle."

"Come on," said Dad. "The rain's getting worse. Let's get home."

The rain was so thick it would have been easy to get lost if you didn't know the hill. As they came down to the forest track, a figure loomed out of the rain.

It was Angus standing in the shelter of the trees.

There was no way around him without passing close by. Angus took one look at the eagle in Dad's arms. It was hard to know what he was thinking.

Dad didn't even look at Angus and walked on past.

Granny glared at him as she passed. "What kind of man shoots an eagle? You should go to prison for this."

"Give up," said Angus. "You've got no proof."

The rain came down harder around them. Angus turned and vanished into the dark spaces between the trees. Bobbie watched him go. It just wasn't right. Someone had to protect the eagles.

"I won't give up," Bobbie yelled after him. "I'll never give up."

*

Mum had put the kettle on, and she'd got out dry towels for them and another dry blanket for the eagle.

Uncle Fraser looked up from his phone. "The eagle watchers will be here in about an hour. They said to keep the eagle warm and wrapped with a hood to calm it." He picked up an old sock with a hole cut in the end. "This might fit."

Bobbie slipped it over the eagle's head and the bird seemed to relax.

"I've got a large box we can put it in," said Mum.

Bobbie sat down beside the eagle and waited for the eagle watchers.

Uncle Fraser came to sit beside her. "I've never seen an eagle up close," he said. "I've seen stuffed ones at the museum, but this is different, isn't it? Seeing it right in front of you. Just look at the size of those talons."

Bobbie nodded. It was as if the mountains and moorland were wrapped up in this fierce wild bird.

Granny pulled up a chair. "We need eagles here. They belong here. We'd have more if they weren't killed on grouse moors. It's not just here. They're killed on other moors in Scotland as well."

"Don't eagles take lambs too?" said Uncle Fraser.

"Not if you're a good shepherd," said Bobbie proudly. "Healthy ewes defend their lambs."

"But what if the eagles took some of them?" said Uncle Fraser. "I'm sure even a great shepherd couldn't look after them all."

Bobbie looked at the eagle. "But the world is not just about us, is it? It belongs to the eagles too. What kind of world would we have if we lost all the wild?"

"Isn't that the truth?" said Granny. "And no amount of books or culture can teach you that.

You have to feel it. You have to be connected to the earth to feel it."

"Oh, Granny. It's not one or the other," said Bobbie. "We can have both. I love being here and seeing the eagles, but I also love hearing about the Kazakh nomads who hunt with eagles. There's nothing to stop you reading Uncle Fraser's books too."

Granny looked down at her hands. "Yes, there is," she said softly.

"What?" asked Bobbie.

"Well, I don't read so well," said Granny. "I never have done."

Uncle Fraser laughed. "Don't be daft. Of course you can read."

Granny looked up at him. "No," she said. "I hid it well. See, not even my brother knew. It's not something you want people to know."

Mum put a hand on Granny's arm.

Granny shook it off. "Even when the school opened again, I couldn't learn to read. I don't know why. I just couldn't. No one helped me. Everyone laughed at me and even the teacher told me I was stupid. You learn to hide these things."

"Granny!" said Bobbie. "I didn't know."

But Granny pulled on her hat, pushed her hands deep in her pockets and was already on her way out of the door.

Uncle Fraser's phone buzzed. "The eagle watchers are here. They're coming up the track."

Mum let the eagle watchers in. Their names were Rachel and Tom.

Rachel bent down to the eagle. She ran her fingers across the soft feathers of its head and then she checked the satellite tag and the number on the ring around its leg. She frowned. "This one's called Skye," she said. "I was the one who fitted his ring and tag last year when he was six weeks old."

"We heard shots in the night," said Bobbie.

"That's often the way now," said Tom. "We think eagles are killed at night so no one can see who does it. It means we've got no proof and whoever does it gets away with murder."

Rachel gently lifted Skye up and stretched his wings. "Doesn't look like his wings are broken, but I suspect there's shot inside him. An X-ray will show it."

"We'd better take him to the vet," said Tom.

Bobbie walked with them to their car. She wanted to fetch Granny but could see the eagle watchers didn't want to hang around.

Before they drove away, Bobbie said, "Will you let me know what happens to him? I need to know."

"Of course," smiled Rachel. "He wouldn't be alive if it wasn't for you."

Chapter 11

Over the next few days, Bobbie didn't want to go out on the moor in case she met Angus. She stayed at home with her sheep. Granny stayed at home too and didn't say much to anyone. She'd lost her spark. It was as if the fierce fire that burned inside her had gone out. She sat outside her shed just staring into space. She didn't want to come on walks around the farm with Bobbie and she didn't even comment on Uncle Fraser when he drank from teacups or ate from the best china.

At breakfast one morning, Uncle Fraser cut his toast in triangles and sighed. "I wish I'd seen the eagle flying," he said. "I've never seen a real bird of prey flying free like that in the wild."

"Well, you're out of luck. There's none around here," grumbled Granny. "Angus sees to that. We should have eagles and hen harriers and peregrine falcons and owls and red kites. But they're killed the moment they fly over the grouse moor."

"We could take Uncle Fraser to see the ospreys at Jamie's Pond," said Bobbie. "You can take a wheelchair up there too, so it won't matter that he can't walk very far."

"Ospreys?" said Uncle Fraser. "Do you mean those birds of prey that catch fish from the water? I've always wanted to see them."

Granny nodded. Something seemed to come alive in her again. "I'm sure Jamie would let us in."

Jamie was a local farmer who owned trout pools. The ospreys came so often to catch fish that he made more money from charging people to photograph the birds than he did from charging people who wanted to come and fish.

Dad drove them to Jamie's farm. He helped Uncle Fraser into the bird hide.

"We won't have to wait long," whispered Granny. She pointed up to the sky where an osprey was circling overhead, showing the pale underside of its body. It was a big bird with huge wings. Bobbie could see the brown eye stripe as it turned its head to look into the water.

Swirls on the top of the pond were the only clue that fish swam beneath.

"Now," whispered Granny.

The osprey swooped low and came in for the dive. It flew down over the water. At the last moment its legs swung forwards and its talons plucked a fish from the water. It flew upwards and behind the hide. A massive trout thrashed and wriggled in the osprey's talons as it flew.

Uncle Fraser's eyes were shining all the way home. "Amazing," he kept saying. "Simply amazing."

"Just think if we had wild eagles and people came to our farm to see them?" said Bobbie.

"I know," said Granny. "Think how many birds of prey we'd have if Angus didn't kill them."

They drove home in silence after that.

*

At home, Bobbie went out to help Dad with the sheep.

They climbed to the highest hill on the farm and looked out across the moors to the mountains beyond.

"Do you think we'll have eagles again?" asked Bobbie.

"Maybe," said Dad. "There are some places in Scotland where they have stopped shooting grouse and are letting the wild come back."

"I hope that happens here," said Bobbie. She watched the cloud shadows slide across the valley floor. The river glittered gold in the evening light and the sky was tinted with pink.

This was her world, where she wanted to be. She didn't want to have to leave, ever.

"I love it here, Dad," she said.

He smiled and put his arm around her. "Me too."

She wanted to tell him that she didn't want to go to a school far away from here, but she didn't dare. She didn't want to hear what he might say.

Bobbie and Dad walked home in the gathering dark. Dew was settling on the ground and a chill was in the air. They passed close by to Granny's shed and could smell wood smoke. Bobbie stopped for a moment, hidden in the trees. Granny and Uncle Fraser were sitting in deckchairs by the campfire, blankets over their knees. Candles glowed in the twilight.

Uncle Fraser was holding a book in his hands. "Now, this is a story I think you'd like to hear," he said to Granny. "It's one of my favourites. The girl in the story reminds me of you. It's called *The Snow Goose*."

And in the cool evening, surrounded by the purple moors and mountains, and warmed by the glow of flames from the fire, Uncle Fraser sat reading a story to his sister about a girl who saved a snow-white goose.

*

At supper that evening, Mum cooked lasagne, Bobbie's favourite. Granny and Uncle Fraser sat at the same end of the table chatting like old friends.

Mum put garlic bread on the table. "Well, if there's one good thing that's come from all this, it's seeing you two getting on."

"I know," said Uncle Fraser. "Seems like we've a lot of catching up to do."

"And I'll put on my posh town coat and come to see you in Edinburgh," said Granny. She turned to Bobbie. "I'll come and visit you at St Rhona's too."

"But, Granny—" began Bobbie.

Granny put her hand in the air. "Fraser's right. School is important. I didn't have the choice when I was your age, but Fraser is offering it to you."

"But I don't want to go away," said Bobbie.

"It won't be for ever," said Mum. "You can come home in the holidays."

Bobbie put her knife and fork down and looked around at them all. "Uncle Fraser," she said, "it's really kind of you to offer to pay for me to go to St Rhona's. But I don't want to go."

"Give yourself time to think about it," said Dad.

"I have," said Bobbie. "I know what I think. Granny didn't have the choice when she was younger, but I do. We have good schools here too. My friends are here. I want to stay here, on the farm. It's my choice. It's what I choose to do."

Uncle Fraser dabbed his mouth with his napkin. He looked a bit down-hearted. "I can see why you love it here so much. You are more like your granny than you know." He sighed. "I suppose I hoped I'd see more of you if you were in Edinburgh."

"I'd love to go with Granny and see you in Edinburgh," said Bobbie. "You could show us the museums and the galleries."

"And you'll have to come here more often to see us," said Granny.

Uncle Fraser smiled. "Well, I'd love to come back. Maybe you'll have eagles back here too."

Bobbie helped herself to more garlic bread. "That would be a dream come true."

"Talking of dreams," Dad said. "Dougie McKenzie rang to say his sheepdog has had a litter of pups."

Bobbie's eyes opened wide. "Can we get one?"

"Maybe," said Dad. He glanced at Granny and chuckled. "Dougie's father isn't so keen on you having one of his pups. He's still not forgotten Granny beating him and his brother nearly fifty years ago at the sheepdog trials. He said if Bobbie ends up as good a shepherd as Granny, she'll beat them all the time."

Granny grinned. "When do we get started?"

Bobbie felt tears rush to her eyes. She wanted to hug them all, but she didn't want them to see her cry. Instead, she rushed up to her bedroom, where she let the tears fall. She pressed her face against the window and looked out across the fields and the moors and the heather.

Maybe dreams really could come true.

She could stay here, at home.

She was going to have a sheepdog of her very own.

Maybe there would be eagles soaring over the farm one day too.

Chapter 12

Bobbie and Granny sat in the back of the Land Rover as it bumped over the track. Tom and Rachel, the eagle watchers, sat in the front, and Rachel steered the Land Rover over the rocky ground.

Bobbie couldn't help looking back at the box with breathing holes. The eagle, Skye, was inside. It had been six weeks since Bobbie had rescued him. Tom said the X-rays had shown that lead shot had hurt Skye's wing, but that no bones had been broken. They'd looked after Skye for nearly six weeks, and now he was ready to be let go.

The early autumn air was crisp and bright. A week of good weather was forecast too, which gave Skye plenty of opportunity to hunt.

The eagle watchers had decided to release Skye away from the grouse moor to a place they knew he had visited before.

"He spent many months here," said Rachel. "It's near to the nest where he was hatched. He knows this landscape well."

"What if he flies back over the grouse moor?" said Bobbie.

Tom sighed. "It's a risk eagles face. All we can do is to keep them as safe as we can."

"They'll be safe on our farm," said Bobbie fiercely. "I'll watch out for him."

Rachel nodded. "We need more eagle warriors like you to fight for all birds of prey."

"Is that what we are?" asked Bobbie. "Eagle warriors?"

Rachel smiled. "Of course. There's a whole army of people out there wanting to protect them too."

Bobbie frowned. "But how do you stop people like Angus? There's no proof he did it. He or the duke won't go to jail."

"It's why we keep fighting," said Tom. "It's why we put satellite tags on the eagles. When they vanish over a grouse moor, a pattern is showing up. People are beginning to work out what's happening. We're losing our birds of prey on grouse moors like this across the country. It's a national disgrace."

Rachel stopped the Land Rover at the end of the track and Tom got out and poured tea from a Thermos flask for everyone. "Let Skye settle a bit from the bumpy ride before we take him out."

Bobbie watched the eagle warriors pull on their woolly hats and old coats. She leaned into Granny. "They're not your typical warriors."

Granny smiled. "No. But then again, neither are we."

"Right," said Tom. "We'll release Skye over there." He pointed to the top of a hill where the wind rose up from the valley. "Skye will get a good view of the land from up there. And there's plenty of food about."

"We've put a dead deer's body out for him to eat while he builds up his strength," said Rachel.

They all walked up to the hill where Tom put the box on the ground. He handed Bobbie a pair of leather gloves. "Would you like to be the one to let him go?"

"Me?" said Bobbie. "Can I?"

"You saved him," said Tom. "I think it should be you."

"It's only right," said Granny. "You and this eagle have a bond now."

Bobbie pulled on the gloves while Tom opened the box and lifted Skye out. There was a hood over his head to keep him calm.

"Just mind the feet," said Tom. "The talons can really hurt. The beak isn't so bad."

Bobbie held the feet together in one hand and folded her other arm around the eagle's wings.

"I'm going to take the hood off now," said Rachel. "Just hold tight for the moment."

Rachel slipped the hood from Skye's head and Bobbie could feel the eagle tense up. She could feel his wings strain against her and his strong legs trying to pull free from her grip. He scanned the sky and the valley beyond.

Bobbie felt a fierce love for him. This bird had brought her family together. He had taught her to be brave and stand up for herself. Now he fought to return to the wild sky.

A sudden gust of wind rushed up from the valley.

"Now," Tom said.

Bobbie bent her knees and used all her strength to throw Skye up into the air. He exploded from her arms and his huge wings pushed the air back in her face.

He flapped hard until he caught the rising thermals and flew higher and higher until all they could see was his dark shape against the sun.

Bobbie smiled and closed her eyes. She spread her arms wide like wings, feeling for the wind as it tugged at her coat and lifted the ends of her hair. And in that one moment, it felt as if the world had dropped away and she too was high in the air above the mountains.

She was soaring with the eagle, flying high and flying free.

Our books are tested
for children and young people by
children and young people.

Thanks to everyone who consulted on
a manuscript for their time and effort in
helping us to make our books better
for our readers.